The Black Diamond Mystery

The Black Diamond Mystery

Maria Aparecida Cerri

Library of Congress Control Number:		2018913687
ISBN:		
	Hardcover	978-1-9845-6655-3
	Softcover	978-1-9845-6654-6
	eBook	978-1-9845-6653-9

Print information available on the last page.

Rev. date: 11/21/2018

To order additional copies of this book, contact:
Xlibris
1-888-795-4274
www.Xlibris.com
Orders@Xlibris.com
782205

She was very fast. She needed to escape those men. No one, not a single soul, appeared to help her. Occasionally, she looked back, fearing to be caught, but she could deceive those horsemen well. Suddenly, she found herself in a sinister place: a huge castle that gave the impression that she had returned in time. It was so great its towers seemed to reach for the sky!

"It is here," she thought out loud, "here that I will hide."

She approached the great bridge and went for help. The moment she had just crossed it, they lifted the bridge in time for her to escape.

"Where did she go?" shouted one of them.

But no one had seen her.

"Is anyone there?" yelled the girl.

But she did not get an answer. She started to walk toward the castle. She crossed a lake where there were some swans swimming; it was really tranquil. She observed the place. The day was cloudy, gloomy, and gray; but it was pleasing to the eyes. The trees were an invitation to arrival, and at that moment, along with the wind, a ballet of dry leaves could be seen. The wind show took several minutes. Some of the pine trees bended, reaching the ground. After everything calmed down, Cristina saw behind the castle a chain of mountains.

It was a wonderful sight! It gave her the impression that she had stepped into a work of art.

She didn't stop to think about who had lowered the bridge for her to pass. Arriving at one of the entrances, she took a deep breath and shyly debated about knocking or not on the door. It was only opened after the third try. She then put her head inside, checking the place out.

"Hello!"

She didn't hear any answer.

"Is there anybody there?"

Only after a few minutes, someone came to meet her. She couldn't believe her eyes.

"Don't be scared, young lady. Here, you'll be safe."

She rubbed her eyes to check what she was seeing.

"You . . . do you speak?"

"Don't be worried, young one. I'll not sweep you from here."

"Are you a . . . ?"

"Oh, that don't bother me anymore. I have other partners in more embarrassing situations." And he continued, "How did you get here?"

"I was looking—"

Cristina heard a voice behind her.

"Sit down here! You must be tired."

She looked and saw a very plump and pleasant chair! Its arms held her by the waist, making her sit down.

"Sit on my lap for a little bit," said the chair.

She rubbed her eyes one more time to see if she could believe what she was seeing there. It was not possible; she must have been delirious. Cristina then began to think about the idea of having entered a haunted castle. But they seemed to be so sweet! Cristina heard a murmur behind her. It seemed that someone whispered something in her ear, but someone blew the chandelier just in time.

"I just wanted to cuddle," he told his companion, who was beside him.

"It's all right," said Cristina, "if this is the normal way to receive a person!"

At this moment, a woman went through a hallway in front of Cristina.

"Hey, could you help me?" she asked. "What's happening around here?"

The woman quickened her steps and didn't look. Once again, Cristina asked, but the woman, without showing her face, said that she should be careful and that if she still had time, she should go back to the place where she came from.

"Why would you be telling me this?"

"Girl, run! It's very dangerous. Get away from here before she sees you."

"Who is she?"

The woman, however, did not respond and disappeared in a hurry. Cristina went to the door and tried to do the knob, but it was too late. She could not open it. She tried to leave again but to no avail. At that moment, she saw a young man with a funny hat on his head passing through a corridor. From far away, she asked him to help her get out, but he did not care. It seemed that he didn't hear her. She decided to follow him, quickening her steps a little more, and she saw when he entered a golden cage and went up.

The place was huge! The place was huge! It could house many families there. Then the cage came back down again, empty.

She wondered if she should enter it or not, but she needed to find him to ask from help. The cage went up with the girl inside. Wherever she passed, there were halls, chapels, and big rooms, all in absolute silence. Suddenly, the cage stopped. She continued to look for the guy to ask for information, but she did not see him.

Strange, she thought. *A place like this and I can't see anybody! Where are the people who live here?*

She walked down the corridors and saw a huge bird singing in the windowsill. She approached it carefully until she came close. She was amazed by its singing. She seemed to know the bird. As she tried to caress his feathers, he flew out the window.

"Come back here. I do not want to do you any harm!" she said, yet she only saw him as he landed on another tree.

She spent a long time there looking out the window and at the landscape surrounding the castle. She was isolated from the world, surrounded by mountains and woods. She saw nothing else. It was about to get dark, so remembering the guy, she decided to look for him again. She crossed the hall and started up a staircase. A great noise shook the castle. Cristina could not stand anymore and rolled down the stairs.

"What's happening!" screamed the girl.

She tried to go up again, but it was in vain. The castle continued to rock from side to side, like an inflatable balloon, and at the same time, the wind whistled, the wall clock played nonstop music, and a chorus of voices came from the party hall. It was all very magical! She covered her ears, for there was too much information for her eardrums. After a few minutes, everything went silent. She sat down on the stairs to rest. Who could be the author of all that?

The song continued, and Cristina walked toward the choir. It was a beautiful classic. Cristina remembered her parents, and she missed them. Where could they be now? Why did they disappear to without warning? They had never done anything like it, but she would find them and was willing to go to the end of the world to save them if she had to. She had inherited this courage from her father, who was determined and brave. Nothing made him fear.

The music woke her up again, and she got close to the door. She was happy because she would find people to talk to, and she began to think she was safe in there. Slowly, she opened the door and saw the room was slightly dark. The music stopped, leaving everything in total silence.

"Where are you?" asked Cristina. "Why did you stop the music?"

Cristina walked in, looked from one side to the other, and saw a little animal that looked like a fennec fox (the smallest of all existing foxes), with ears so huge that they were about fifteen centimeters long. The other companions were frightened and hidden behind a large wooden trunk and only putting their heads out.

"Oh! You don't need to be scared! Who are you? What are you doing here?" she asked without getting any answer.

There was a piano in a corner, with music sheets. She touched a key, and the little animals hid themselves.

"Sorry, I didn't want to scare you!"

She sat in a seat and began to talk to the little animals. Were they lost like her? She held one of the animals in her arms and petted it. She got distracted doing that and lost count of the time. She fell into a deep sleep and only woke up when the sun came through the window. She jumped up and said, "My god, what am I doing here?"

She remembered what had happened the day before. She went to the window to get some fresh air. She was really hungry. Where would she find food? Desolate and not knowing what to do, she returned to look for the little animals. When Cristina looked, she found a table full of food. She didn't think twice. She advanced to the food with all fury. Only then did she realize that she might have touched something that was not hers. In fact, she did not have these bad habits, but the hunger had spoken louder. But who would have prepared that delicious banquet? She walked around the room, looking for the fennec foxes. Were they the ones who had prepared that banquet? Impossible! At this moment, she heard a voice that said, "You don't need to be embarrassed! The banquet was for you."

"Who is there? Come up!"

She was shaking. She walked around the room, looking for the owner of that voice, but she didn't see anybody. She knew then, for sure, that the castle was under a spell. She left the room and went down the stairs. Once again, the young man went through very fast, like a flash. It looked like they were playing hide-and-seek. "What made him walk so much from one side to the other?" Cristina thought aloud.

The clock played a song, indicating the time. Twelve strikes.

She reached a window from which came a noise, and the movement outside drew her attention. Knights were dragging a shirtless man that had his hands tied. What had happened to him?

I'd better be careful, or I might be next, Cristina thought.

She continued to walk through the chambers of the castle, and suddenly, she saw a very brave dwarf with a man who was five times bigger than him. Next to them, there was a silver barrel that shone like a mirror. The little dwarf put something inside it, but the man took it out. What were they doing? It was a very strange situation. She came a little closer to see what it was, but the glass wall did not let her through. She made signs and shouted, but they did not hear her.

Christina then decided to leave and continue to look for the young man because her intuition told her that he was the only one who could help her. She climbed a few steps and entered a hall. The castle began to rock softly. The objects moved back and forth. At that moment, she thought it was even fun. The castle stopped shaking. Cristina took a deep breath, for she was dizzy. She got up, walked down the hall, and saw the young man with the funny-looking hat go by. She called him, but he didn't pay attention, like he couldn't hear her. She decided to follow him without being noticed.

She hid behind a column. She wouldn't go in without knowing the place. At that moment, she heard a big noise coming from the window.

Cristina shuddered with a loud scream though. "What is that!" One more surprise.

"She is coming!" announced a voice. "Hide yourselves!"

"The choir! Why is it not singing?" asked the guy.

The scene she watched was very strange. Through the window came a dark-green-and-brown dragon with huge wings and red eyes like embers. The dragon let out a sharp cry that almost deafened her. It carried on its back a woman in a purple dress with a black hood. Her hair, black and thin, fell down to her waist. Her hands, so white, looked like wax, and on her ring finger was something that caught Cristina's attention. *The ring!* Cristina thought, because it looked like her mother's ring. The woman had a thin face and strong eyes. She got down from the dragon with great agility and began to walk around the room, giving orders to the young man. She strongly used the whip she had in her hands. It almost made the castle shake, yet that was the signal for the choir to begin singing.

"That's much better!" she said. "I've already told you that every time I arrive, I want to see you singing in tune."

She sat in a chair and seemed to relax to the music. On a wall, there was a large mirror, and when the music ended, the woman approached it and entered, like in a magic pass.

How did she do that? thought Cristina. *It must be a trick. I want to see how she can get out of there.*

Hours later, the woman came out of the mirror and snapped her fingers in its direction, like she was locking it.

"Abel!" screamed the woman.

In a moment, the young man with the funny-looking hat came in.

Ah! His name is Abel, thought Cristina.

After talking to him for a long time, everything became silent, and the woman went down using the golden cage. She went to the kitchen reserved for her and prepared something to eat.

Cristina couldn't participate in that scene because she did not want to leave the place where she was. She felt safe there, but she imagined the woman stirring a big cooking pot of soup made with strange ingredients, as every witch does. Quickly, Cristina went to the room and observed every detail, including the details of the wall. She approached the mirror but did not see anything unusual about it. She saw her reflection in the mirror and straightened her hair.

How did she enter the mirror? Cristina thought. She went to the table and saw the ring on top of it. She picked it up and saw the inscription of her mother's name inside it.

It's impossible! How did she get the ring? Then she thought, *My parents are around here. She must have done something to them.*

She left the ring where she had found it and went back to her hiding place. She would find out what was happening in that place. When the woman came up again, she called the young man, who answered her quickly.

She asked him for a drink and, after that, for him to prepare her bath. Quickly, the man left, and even faster, he arrived with the drink in his hand, like magic.

"This is really good," the woman said as she laughed. "Don't you want to try it?" She spoke sarcastically.

Cristina continued to hide herself in a corner while listening to everything. It felt like she was in a dream from which she would wake up at any minute. And it was like that all the time. The guy came in and out all the time, bringing things to the room. And when everything was quiet, Cristina fell asleep while sitting down in that place. The next day, she was awoken by someone touching her shoulders.

"Hey, young lady, what are you doing here?"

Cristina was scared, She looked at the man, rubbed her eyes, and put her hand over her mouth, yawning.

"Where am I? What place is this?"

The guy stopped her. "How did you end up here?"

"Excuse me! I did not want to break into anyone's house. I don't even know how I got here. I was looking for my parents who disappeared, and when I approached, someone lowered the bridge for me to pass. Wasn't it you?"

"Me? Of course not, but I suspect I know who it was. She lives on the windowsill to see what goes on outside and dreams of someone who'll come to free us."

"Free you?"

"Yes! We are prisoners. Nobody can get out of here."

"But why? What happened?"

"This is a long and dangerous story. It's better that you don't learn it now. You look like a good person, then I'll only ask you to be careful and that you don't let her see you."

"Who? The woman who arrived on a dragon?"

"Did you see her?" he asked, surprised.

"Yes. When she entered the room. Who is she?"

"Her name is Zena. She imprisoned us. You can't appear while she is around. It'll be your end is this happens. What do you want here?"

Cristina then explained to the guy how she had gotten to the castle and that she was looking for her parents. They had mysteriously disappeared since the day they left for a tournament, but she had paid no attention to the place of the competition. When she decided to look for them, asking whomever she would find around—at train stations, at churches, at parks—nobody had seen them. She talked about the men who had chased her until she had entered the castle and saved herself.

"Abe, why do you use this strange hat?"

"She could kill me if I took it off."

"Zena?"

"Yes. This hat is to show that I owe her my obedience."

"She has my mother's ring. I'm sure it's the same."

"Didn't your parents disappear? Then don't doubt that she has also made them prisoners."

"I'll find out," Cristina said. "I only wanted to know why she is doing so many bad things."

"Just to do bad things. There is no other reason," said Abel.

"Why are things here so strange? Objects that can talk, a choir that is not formed by people, a castle that moves, but doesn't fall . . . how can all this happen?"

"It's a mystery!" Abel said. "This castle has belonged to my family for generations, but it is now under Zena's control. She controls the whole region, exploiting people with slavery work. I feel sorry for whomever disobeys her. Of everything the people own, half goes to her. In the field, half of the harvest belongs to her. The one who refuses to pay is punished. One word that defines her is *ambition*. After she took power, no one had peace anymore. However, her biggest ambition is to find the Black Diamond."

"Black Diamond?"

"Yes!"

"And to whom does it belong?"

"The Black Diamond was the king's greatest treasure. It disappeared, and nobody knows how. When people learned of this treasure, they began a fierce race to find it at any cost, but no one ever heard of it again.

"Zena was the most perverse of them. It was another day of tournament inside the castle. It was on that day that everything happened. The knights were in armor, spears, and shields and were preparing to fight one another. Her plan was infallible. Luckily, there were not many people in the place that day. They were cheering for the agility of the riders, for they were all very skillful and wanted to show it. But among them, one stood out, leaving the others wounded. And in the end, she took off his mask and asked, 'Did you like it?' Everyone was surprised. They wanted to know where that woman had come from, and at that moment, she put the spell on everyone. She did all this for revenge."

"Revenge?" asked Cristina.

"Yes. That's all I know."

"What about you? Where were you?"

"Traveling, and when I returned, I found everything as you see. I don't know yet what to do or if anything can be done to defeat her. Zena's threats are enormous, and there are lots of people in danger."

"Have you ever sought help from someone?"

"How? Nobody can leave this place. I have an aunt who lives far away, and only she can help us. I don't know how to get there because we are watched all the time."

"There must be a way," Cristina said. "In life, there's a solution for everything. We need to save them."

"I've already told you that we are watched. Besides that, if she finds you here, she'll hurt you. I'm telling you. If you want to help, it's better to be careful and not show up when she's around."

"But we have to do something. We can't cross our arms," said Cristina.

"I've thought of everything. She's dangerous and knows how to use her power."

"We have to find a way to get out of here and ask for help. Spells don't last forever. This woman is not invincible," Cristina said.

"You are right. Together we can defeat her."

Abel asked that for now, she would remain hiding in the bedroom and avoid walking around the castle. That way, she wouldn't risk being found by Zena. It was unknown if that was part of the magic, but she didn't appear every night, only when there was no moon in the sky. And soon enough, before the sun came up, she was far away. But whenever she appeared, making all that noise, Christina was well hidden in her corner. She could hear the choir, the noise of the wind that stirred the whole castle, and the orders given to Abel.

As the days went by, Abel and Cristina became good friends. Her life inside the castle was reduced to finding a way to get out of there without being noticed and to ask for help to break the spell. Once, they tried, using a long rope, to get out through one of the towers; however, when Abel went down the rope, a strange animal had it cut. By little, he didn't hit the ground. It was hard to explain to Zena the reason why he was hurt. Another time, he tried to leave using a disguise, but he was discovered. And even worse, he was punished by Zena.

On a rainy afternoon, Cristina was alone in the bedroom, thinking and trying to find a way out. All of a sudden, she had an idea. It was risk, she concluded, but it was the best one she had so far. She had to think positively because it had to go right. She called Abel, who came running.

"What? What happened?" he asked, frightened.

"I know what to do!"

She then explained her plan that, by the way, was very insane.

"Are you crazy? Do you have any idea what can happen to you if she finds you?"

"It was the best that came to my mind. We have to try, otherwise, we'll be stuck here for the rest of our lives. Now that everything is planned, I won't give up."

Cristina was a very determined and persistent. When she put something in her head, that was it.

"But it's too dangerous!" Abel said.

"I know that, but that's the way life is: full of risks. If I don't try, there's no way to know if it'll work. I need you to tell me about the person that can help us."

"Aunt Lobélia?" asked Abel.

"Yes. Where does she live?"

He explained the way she would have to go to get to her house.

It would not be easy because it was far away, and it involved danger and risks. He draw a map and put an X on a hill the top of a hill, indicating the place, and he gave it to Cristina.

"Good luck, Cristina. I hope that your plan works. If there was any way I could go too . . . but Zena would miss me, and that would put everything to lose."

"If I can get out of here safe and alive, I will get to your aunt's house. Let's see what she'll say."

There were no stars in the sky that night, and Zena appeared. Abel went to serve her as usual, preparing her drink and a bath with herbs. The bath took a long time; it seemed like a kind of ritual. After that, he prepared a strange-looking soup and pleased her in every way he could. On that day, he was even gentler than usual. She asked for a drink and looked decided on getting drunk. After that, she had the soup and fell into a deep sleep.

Abel went to the room where Cristina was and called her to say that the moment to put the plan in practice had arrived. They went to the place where the dragon that, by luck, was always sleeping was. They then very carefully tied a rope around one of its legs and then to Cristina's waist. As a precaution, Abel gave her a dagger.

"Are you sure you don't want to give up on this crazy idea?"

"Come on! I'm not one to give up like that."

He wished her good luck. When everything was under absolutely silence, Zena woke up.

"It looks like I've slept for one hundred years! Am I late? Let's go!"

She sat at the animal's back, and they left through the window, with Cristina tied to one of the dragon's legs. As they passed through the window, the dragon got stuck. He didn't want to keep going.

"What's happening to you?" yelled Zena.

Abel, who watched the scene from a distance, feared for Cristina. Now she was going to see her. Zena whipped the dragon, and fortunately, it flew outside the window. Cristina thought and planned the right moment to get out of there without being noticed. She was always careful and alert. And of course, with its size, the dragon couldn't feel the girl holding to its leg, as she was as like a fly touching its skin. If Cristina didn't feel so jeopardized, the trip could have been fun. But she had pay attention to where Zena would stop.

Along the way, they passed through a huge plantation, and Zena asked the dragon to blow. The fire spread throughout the field. From above, Cristina only saw the light from the fire while Zena laughed hard. *Such evil!* she thought. *I'm not going to be able to handle so much destruction.*

After a long time of crossing the skies and cutting off wind and clouds, the dragon descended (probably) in their usual place. The landscape was deserted and gothic. The civilization was left behind. Zena left, leaving the dragon at the entrance of a very strange and somber place. Dried trees were visible, and even in the dark, it seemed that they were alive. Some owls seemed to seek their pray at dawn. There was a stone gate in the supporting wall with a statue of a woman. The day dawned, and some stars still glowed in the sky. Below, the horizon line timidly began to turn orange.

At that instant, Cristina saw it was the right moment to leave. She tried to cut the rope with the dagger, but she couldn't. She turned from side to side, but she didn't get anywhere. She was trapped under the dragon, which didn't move because it was too big. She tried many times without success. She was like a fly trying to move. Cristina started to get desperate. She got the dagger and stuck it on the dragon's paw. Letting out a scream of pain and sending fire in every direction, the dragon finally lifted its paw. Cristina then used that opportunity to run without being noticed and hide behind a tomb. How luck! The dragon sent out flames that reached old tombstones. Cristina kept still and unmoving. Then she saw that the place was an old cemetery. She wasn't scared; she was only worried about the dragon, which was her only real danger at the moment.

The dragon was furious. Hearing its scream, Zena came to see what had happened.

"What happened, my little pet? You always stay here by yourself. This is your place. Did you forget it?"

She checked him, moving from one place to the next like a sniffer dog, and she saw the sliced rope on the side.

"What is this? Who was here?"

Cristina curled up as much as she could and prayed that she wasn't discovered. She would be lost if that happened. After everything had calmed down and she saw that she was no longer in danger because Zena was no longer around, she realized where she was. At that moment, the sun was already high in the sky. She crossed the cemetery to find her way out of there. She couldn't go through where the dragon was. She walked over fallen crosses, broken tombs, and candles scattered around tombstones; and she continued until she found a way out.

What a relief, she thought. She sat outside under a tree to rest a bit, then she decided to return to her trip. As she went down a little hill, she saw a growling dog coming in her direction.

She was paralyzed. She took a deep breath and controlled her breathing, as if she wasn't afraid. *One more thing,* Cristina thought.

"Easy!" Cristina said in a low voice. "I won't hurt you."

The dog growled in her direction, showing his enormous teeth. Moved by the adrenaline, Cristina climbed anywhere she could. The dog lowered its ears and stopped growling. *What happened to him?* Cristina asked herself.

At that moment a voice yelled, "Thunder! Let's go!"

When she turned, she saw a redheaded woman coming from the other direction. She carried something in her arms. She got closer, greeted her, and said, "Is this your dog?"

"He's following me," answered the woman.

They walked through the green hill and stopped in front of a cabin surrounded by trees. It was so fresh!

"I'm very thirsty," said Cristina.

"Right there, there's a faucet with water. It's refreshing and clear," said the woman.

Cristina didn't think twice and ran there. She drank a lot of water.

"Ah! How good it is to quench the thirst!"

The woman, who was eating, offered a piece of bread to Cristina, who accepted and thanked her. The bread was delicious, different from any other she had eaten. After eating, Cristina opened the map and quietly observed it. Then she thought out loud.

"Mrs. Lobélia . . ."

"Mrs. Lobélia, do you know her?" asked the woman excitedly.

"Do I know her? No, I don't. But I need to find her. I'm looking for her."

"I'm going there too," said the woman. "I'm taking my little daughter, who is sick. I can show you the way."

"What's wrong with your daughter?"

The woman showed her the child. It was a little girl with a face and lips so pale that you couldn't say if she was alive. For a minute, Cristina felt a shiver with what she was seeing. But she didn't have the courage to make any comments. They both stayed in silence, each thinking about their destination. After a few minutes, the woman broke the silence:

"If we want to get there, we have a long walk ahead of us."

They continued on the way to Aunt Lobélia's house. They walked so much that they lost count of the days. They faced sun, rain, and cold. They crossed a vast forest with gigantic trees; their twisted branches reached the ground. Only the noise of the animals, of the branches splitting, and of the night bugs could be heard. On a tree branch, an owl hooted, and bats went flying as they got closer. They got scared many times, and Cristina remembered the stories about monsters who lived in the forest that her grandma used to tell her. It looked like they would never find their way out. She feared having to spend the night in there, but that was exactly what happened. Fortunately, she was accompanied by that lady.

"Maybe we'll find a cave to spend the night," said the woman.

They stopped to rest a little on a leafy tree trunk. From a hole in it, a little animal similar to a squirrel came running. The trunk was pretty thick, and they retreated right there.

"We'll be safe here," said the woman.

"I'm afraid of seeing a snake or a puma," said Cristina.

"They won't get closer. Thunder will watch over us."

The dog lay down near the tree trunk. After a few hours, Cristina heard a noise that made her shiver.

"What is this?" the young woman said, startled.

"Quiet! Don't make any noise, my girl," answered the woman.

The noise got closer to where they were. Cristina opened her eyes and kept her ears alert. She saw an enormous flash. It was an animal with two firelights in the place of its eyes.

"What is this?"

"Don't look," said the woman. "You can go blind. Close your eyes."

Cristina wondered who the woman that accompanied her was because even the wind obeyed her when she ordered. Cristina was brave and courageous, but that woman overcame all her challenges.

"It's the Boitatá! Hide your face, and he'll go away," said the woman, making Cristina get out of her thoughts.

But isn't the Boitatá only a legend of the Brazilian folklore? Cristina thought. However, he was right in front of her. The woman said that he only attacked when people set the forest on fire or abused its inhabitants. Thunder and Boitatá had a fight. They made a great noise. When Cristina tried to see, the dog was completely disfigured.

"My god! What is this?" she said in a low voice, hiding her face again.

"Don't do anything bad to him, Thunder," ordered the woman. "He is only checking to make sure we're not destroying his place. Go sit down."

After the animals fought, when everything was calm again, they were able to rest a bit. Cristina was anxious for the day to come so she could leave that place. It seemed like it was the longest night—a winter solstice, when sunrise never came.

When the first sunrays shyly appeared among the trees, Cristina and her companion retook their course and started walking inside the forest until they found a way out. During the day, everything was calm and fearless. Then, they kept going. The fatigue was getting to them, and when the sun disappeared for a moment, it was a blessing to them. They also faced other torments along the way and could not always find a place to hide. After a long time, they saw an exotic place like it was shown in the map, but to get there they would have to cross a bridge made out of wood and cord. As they got closer, they saw that some of boards on it were broken.

"How can we cross it?" asked Cristina "Maybe there is another way to get there."

"We can do it. Come carefully," advised the woman.

"You can go first," Cristina suggested.

The bridge swung from side to side as they moved toward the middle. The woman crossed the bridge with absolute tranquility; it seemed she was weightless.

"Come now! You don't need to be afraid, come!"

Cristina closed her eyes, took a deep breath, and started walking again on the fragile boards. All of a sudden, the cord broke. She screamed and was already flying through the air when the dog held her by the dress. With great effort, he took her out of there. She was so scared that she couldn't breathe. When she left the bridge, she was exhausted. They then stopped a bit to rest.

"We're arriving," said the woman. "It's right there."

To hear that was a relief to Cristina, who was exhausted. They neared a very modest white house with yellow windows.

"It's here," said the woman. "My journey has ended."

Cristina, however, didn't hear what she said. She clapped her hands, and a young woman appeared at the door.

"What do you want?" she asked.

"We want to talk to Mrs. Lobélia. Does she live here?"

"Yes," said the young woman. "Come on in."

"Let's go!" Cristina said to her travel companion, but as she turned, the woman was no longer there. She looked around, trying to see where she was, but she couldn't see her or the dog. The woman had disappeared like smoke in the air.

"Where did she go?" asked Cristina desperately to the girl who was at the door.

However, the young woman in front of her didn't understand what was happening, but she didn't mind, as she was used to receiving people with strange behaviors.

"Didn't you see her?"

"Who?"

"The woman who was with me. She was with me for the whole trip."

"But you came here alone. There wasn't anybody with you."

"Yes, there was. She was carrying a sick child. I'm not getting crazy yet," Cristina said, getting nervous.

"I'm sorry, but you appeared here by yourself. There wasn't anybody with you. You can come in and wait on that chair if you want," she invited.

Because she didn't want to upset the young woman in front of her, it would do no good to insist. When Cristina entered, she trembled. The child that traveled with her mother was playing with a doll. She looked at Cristina, smiled, and winked at her. Cristina was impressed with that. It was the same girl. *My god!* she thought. *What is happening? What is this mystery that is following me?*

"Whose little child is this?" asked Cristina.

"My cousin. Her mother was Lobélia's daughter. She died when the girl was months old."

"It's impossible. The woman who traveled with me was carrying this girl," said Cristina, already nervous.

"You're tired. That's why you're acting like this. You've traveled a lot, haven't you? When we're tired, we see things that don't exist. We even have hallucinations. Come here, Ana. It's time for you to take your medicine." The young woman took the girl in her arms and left.

Cristina was very impressed with that. The young woman offered her some water and coffee while she waited to be seen. She started looking around the living room, and on the wall, she saw pictures of Saint George, the Sacred Family, Saint Lucy, and the Last Judgment. The Last Judgment's history made her feel a little desperate and distressed, and as she looked at that picture, with angels playing trumpets and the fallen and crying people, it made her think about the histories her grandmother used to tell her about the two paths.

"We only have two paths to follow: the good and the evil. The good one is full of thorns and it's hard to be followed because it is our difficulties, our challenges. And the path of evil is always clean, so it is easier to follow through it. Boys and girls," alerted her grandmother, "always follow the path with the thorns because it's the one that take us to a good place." Of course, it was a symbolic metaphor, as the children could not understand it, especially the reason why they couldn't go through the clean and easy path.

Then she approached another painting. It was one of Saint George, a brave warrior on a white horse with a spear

24

wounding the dragon. She remembered Zena's dragon. It looked the same. Cristina liked it when her father told Saint George's story—a young soldier who faced the dragon to save the people. *How many dragons do the people have to face today?* she thought. *The corruption dragon, the hypocrisy dragon, the capitalism, the greed, the envy* . . .

Suddenly, she was awakened from this memory when the door opened for a woman to leave. She was probably talking to Lobélia.

"It's your turn," invited the young lady. "You can come in! She is waiting for you."

The girl opened the door. She awkwardly approached the woman who was sitting on a chair. The woman was not that young, but she was not old either. What struck Cristina's attention were the sapphires instead of her eyes. They were so blue that they dimmed her vision! She was very fashionable in a dress that matched her eyes and a turban embroidered with tiny stones on her head that showed a little of her reddish hair. Her nails were painted in black, and a ring with a huge stone also demanded attention. But the biggest thing was the resemblance she had to the woman who had accompanied her on the journey there.

"My daughter was a very good and fair person," the woman began. "You don't need to be scared."

Cristina didn't answer anything, mainly because she didn't know what to say, but she had the impression that the woman in front of her knew everything about her life, even her innermost secrets. She wished she could run from there, but it was late.

"You don't need to be overwhelmed, girl! I'm here to counsel you," said the woman.

She asked Cristina to sit on the chair in front of her and started asking questions.

"What brings you here, young lady?"

Cristina looked at Lady Lobélia, evaluating her, and the woman continued, "You're very brave, girl! How many challenges have you faced on the way so far to help people? There is much kindness in your heart! I know how much the people need liberation."

"Do you know Zena?"

"Yes, who don't I know? I know everything that goes on in this place. And Zena went too far with her insanity and her evil."

"What do you do to end her powers? There must be some secret."

"It's to pass through the three doors!"

"Three doors?"

"Yes! Let me explain. Inside the castle, there is a secret tunnel. You and Abel will have to find it and walk through it. Inside, you'll find the three doors. There are many challenges ahead of you. Don't give up, and don't just use your physical strength. Face them with faith, courage, and with your hearts! However, don't take too long because if you don't act fast enough, you'll be imprisoned for the rest of your life. The spell cast there was a very strong one."

Before Cristina left, the woman gave her a bottle with a liquid, a small box, and a golden spear.

"You should open the small box to get into the castle again. As for the other items, keep them safely with you. You'll know the right moment to use them."

Cristina put the items she got inside her clothes.

"Go and tell everything to my nephew, Abel. Tell him to first look for the tunnel I told you about. It ends in one of the bedrooms where the sun rises." After a little pause, she continued, "You were very brave, but you didn't think about how to get back. Do you have any idea?"

"Honestly, I didn't think about this. I have to think about what to do."

"I'm going to ask my helpers to bring you back tomorrow. Today, you can stay here. Ifigênia has already prepared a meal for us. You must be very hungry."

"Yes. I'm really hungry."

After the meal, they talked on the porch and looked at the stars. The woman told her stories, and Cristina listened closely to them. They went to sleep late that evening. The next day, Cristina would leave very early, with the promise of Auntie Lobélia to help her get back.

Cristina woke up with a light and cold rain falling on the roof. It was so good to stay there, but she had to go. She got up, and the two women were already up too. After breakfast, it was the moment to leave. Ifigênia gave her a yellow cape with a hood to help her get protected against the cold. Cristina thanked her for the cape and for the reception and said goodbye to the two women.

"Good luck," said Lady Lobélia.

"We'll need it!"

"We'll take a shortcut," said one of the servants.

Far away, Cristina saw the dog Thunder again, crossing their way.

"Be careful!" she said. "It's Thunder!"

"What was it?" asked one of them.

"Didn't you see a dog?"

"What dog, girl? There isn't any dog here!"

"It seemed like the same one that accompanied me the whole trip."

They walked a little more and found some strange men wearing black capes. They were Zena's men, and they ordered them to stop the carriage.

"Be careful!" said one of them. "They can be robbers."

"That's all I needed now," complained Cristina.

They stopped.

"What are you carrying there?" asked one of them.

"We don't have anything of value. We're coming back from a medical appointment."

"Is the young woman sick? It doesn't look like it."

Cristina was worried about their tone of voice and about what could happen to them. *And this now,* she thought. Those men could cause them harm. Luckily, she wasn't alone. The men made them get down from the carriage and began to search it, looking for something. Whatever they found, they took and put in a bag.

"There's nothing else," said one of them.

"Then, let's take the girl."

They took her and threw her over their shoulders. Cristina kicked and punched them while the men fought. The man was already leaving with Cristina when she screamed, "Catch, Thunder!"

The dog grabbed him by the neck, making him set Cristina free. The dog knocked them down, leaving them wounded. After that, the battle was over, and they continued their journey.

Back at the Castle

The trip back was much shorter, and as they approached the castle, it was already late afternoon. The sun was setting behind the mountains. Cristina looked at the place from far away. The clock on the wall began to sound. The choir began to sing. *It's time for her to arrive,* she thought. They stood there when they saw Zena arriving on top of the dragon.

"What is that?" asked one of them. "I've never seen a scene like this."

"You can go back now," Cristina said.

"But . . . and you? Lady Lobélia said we should protect you. Are you going to be here alone?"

"There's no problem. I have to find a way to enter the castle again."

"Are you sure we can go?"

"Thanks for everything," she said.

Cristina lined the ground and looked in the direction of the castle's window. She imagined everything that was happening at that moment. She didn't see when Zena left, because it was dawn (and at that moment, she was dozing). She had already thought of everything she could do to enter the castle again, but it was watched over by Zena's men. She then remembered the small box that Aunt Lobélia had given her and what she had said: "To get into the castle, you must open the small box."

Was this the moment she should use it? What was in there? There was nothing else to do. Cristina opened the magic box, and it took her flying to the castle's window, like Tinker Bell from Peter Pan. She entered it a little suspicious, looking back and forth. The room was in absolute silence. *Where is Abel?* she thought.

She left that place, went to the hall, and saw the same woman passing by.

"Are you looking for Abel again? Don't you know what happened?"

"What happened to him?" asked Cristina, frightened.

"He's imprisoned on the basement."

"Imprisoned? But why? What has happened?"

"He can explain it to you," said the woman in a low voice.

"And where is this basement?"

"I'll show you, but follow me discretely because if they see you, it could be worse."

The woman gave her a hooded cape to hide in. They went down many stairs until they got to where Abel was. It was a cold and sad place. There were more prisoners with him.

"Abel, what are you doing here?"

"You ask? Who would be the one responsible for this?"

"Why are you imprisoned? What happened?"

"Punishment."

"How? Did she find anything?"

"Somebody told her. Now she is after you."

"I'll get you out of here."

Cristina looked for the keys to open the gate, but she couldn't find it. She couldn't lose any time; each minute was valuable. She looked around the room and in the one next to it until she came back with something in her hand. With a big knife, she cut the lock. They left, running, each one going in a different direction. Abel hugged Cristina, thanking her.

"Tell me everything, Cristina."

"It was a difficult trip, with lots of challenges and mysteries, but so far, everything has been overcome."

She told him everything that had happened on the way, leaving him amazed by her courage. Cristina explained to him in details how they should act. They didn't lose any more time and left to look for the tunnel. They went to the room facing the rising sun and found the door to the passageway.

"We have to go through here," Abel said.

They entered and were certain they were going on the right way.

"We can't lose time if we want to save our families."

It was a little dark, and as they got farther, the tunnel became darker. Occasionally, they heard the flapping of a bat's wings and twined themselves on spiderwebs.

"How didn't I remember it? The flashlight," said Abel, removing it from his pocket.

They spent half of the day looking, without any success.

"How long can this tunnel be?" complained Cristina.

By the end of the afternoon, they were tired of walking, and they saw a light.

"Look, Abel. There's a light at the end of the tunnel!"

They got closer to make sure it was a door. It was locked. They tried to open it, but they couldn't.

"The key! Where is the key?"

Abel took a dagger from this pocket and put it in the door's keyhole. He tried until the door opened. They entered a big dark room with an altar full of burned candles in the middle of it. It looked like a sacred place. Many symbols were painted on the wall! Cristina got distracted while looking at each painting.

"Come on, Cristina, we need to find the other doors. We can't lose any time."

Curious, they opened drawers and looked at the relics, trying hard to guess what they were. There were books written in many languages, tiny statues, bigger statues, and paintings.

"Too many things, Abel!"

"Really, it's a true relic."

Between one search and another, they found a roll of paper tied with a red ribbon. It was a map. They looked at it until something caught their attention. They saw a drawing with three doors: a wooden one, a metal one, and the last one made of crystal that said *Ostium verum*. Next to it, he saw an object that looked like a key. He took it, started to clean it, and put it in his coat.

They wondered how they would go through the three doors.

"Let's go here! Quick!" Abel said, taking Cristina by the arm.

As they approached the wooden door, he examined it first. He then took the key from his pocket and turned it from side to side until he was able to open it. They stood there for a few seconds, fearing that there might be a trap. Then began to search the place. As she approached a box, Cristina gave a startled cry.

"That's horrible! Look, Abel."

"What is it, Cristina?"

She had no time. A huge snake with red eyes and a woman's body started to attack her. Abel took his sword and cut off its head. At the same moment, two heads appeared instead of one. And each time he cut a head, another one appeared. And from its eyes, sparks seemed to come out.

Every time a head was cut, the monster laughed. It seemed like it enjoyed the pain. In its hands, it held a key and pointed to their side. The fight with the huge snake was intense. It was very fast. What would they do to destroy it?

Cristina was getting more and more scared with that scene. She remembered then Lobélia's words—for them to use not only their physical strength but to fight with faith and courage.

"This is the moment," she said.

Taking the bottle from her pocket, she threw the liquid on the snake, and it began to disappear, screaming in pain until it was completely gone. It was one of Zena's secrets. They got close, and with the sword, Abel cut the snake's hand to get the key. They then crossed a long and very narrow hallway that was full of paintings. Cristina stopped to look at them, but Abel pulled her by the arm. They arrived in an enormous room. They entered it and began to look at each object they found.

"Look on that wall!"

"Amazing! It looks real," said Cristina.

It was an enormous sculpture of a tiger embossed on the wall. Cristina got near it and contemplated that figure. She passed her hands over it, as if caressing the sculpture. *Wow! It seems real!* Cristina thought. *Who was the author of this piece of art?*

Meanwhile, Abel looked for the crystal key. They needed to find it as soon as possible, so Cristina decided to leave the sculpture and go to a corner of the room to help him search. They saw a chest full of objects. They looked from one thing to the other, and between them, Abel found a whip made of gold and put it on his waist. At each object found, Cristina became even more amazed and thought about who all that wealth belonged to. Without noticing, Cristina felt a breath on her neck. When she turned, she lost her speech.

Abel saw the enormous beast walking toward him. He tried to remain calm. Where had it come from? *I'm going to have to face it,* he thought. He remembered the whip and started hitting it on the floor. He shouted at the tiger to be firmly at his command. He was caught in that fight for several minutes. Cristina began to return to normal when she noticed that Abel was different. He looked stronger and bigger than he was. His face seemed to have changed. The hat was gone. The tiger roared, and Abel fought it with bravery and cold blood.

"Run, Cristina! Leave me alone with it."

Cristina was worried about leaving him alone, but he yelled again for her to leave that place. It was the best to do. Before Abel's commands, the tiger went back to the wall, immobile and cold as it always was—a sculpture. Abel rested for a few seconds after the fight, took a deep breath, and continued his search to find the last key. It was hanging on the wall next to the tiger. He walked there and took it. At this moment, the tiger gave one more roar and disappeared. He found Cristina next to another door.

"Are you alive?"

"We still have to face the worst beast."

"What beast?"

"The beast of evil!"

They rested a little. Abel gave a satisfied smile—a smile with thirty-two extremely bright pearls. Cristina then realized that he wasn't the same man anymore. He was stronger. The spell seemed to have disappeared. She wanted to talk but couldn't. What had happened?

"Cristina, what happened?"

She didn't listen anymore because she was immersed in that enchantment.

"Let's go, Cristina! We can't lose any more time!"

She shook her head like she could get rid of that image. The last door was the crystal one. It was huge and decorated with golden arabesques.

He put the crystal in a concave place on the door, like the inscription, and soon, it opened. A flash of light almost blinded them. They covered their eyes with their arms and slowly entered. In a huge wooden chair worn by the time was a very skinny and gray-haired woman.

"I'm so glad you came!" said the woman, turning to the two of them.

She turned on the chair. They saw a pale and worn-out face.

"It's me you're looking for, isn't it?"

"Who are you? What are you doing here?" asked Abel.

"I'm here for many springs. I miss the fields, the sun, and the rain," answered the woman with a wick voice.

"Let's go slowly," Cristina said. "You are shaking."

At this moment, a crow appeared and landed on her shoulders. She then said, "Thanks to him, I survived. He's the one who brought me food all this time."

"But what happened for you to be locked in here?" asked Abel.

"So don't you know?"

The woman started to explain the facts.

"You have found the door of truth—the true story that happened. Justice is not done with vengeance and pain but with the truth 'Then you will know the truth, and the truth will set you free.' (That's from the Bible—John 8:32.)"

And the woman continued to talk.

"Zena was raised by me. I found her by the side of the road when she was little. On her neck, she had a little chain with the image of a dragon in it. I thought it wasn't fair for an innocent person to carry such a scary image. I broke the medal immediately. Over the years, I discovered that she was the daughter of a very powerful sorceress who had died in a fire set on her hut. They could only save the girl. They then blamed the king for the crime, but that is not the truth. Zena's mother had a rival who wanted to take her place. She was the one responsible for everything. On that day, one of the king's men passed by the place in the exact moment the tragedy was happening. By luck he was able to save the girl, and he left her by my door.

"I took care of her with love and affection, but when she grew up, she found out what had happened and, thinking that the king was the one responsible, swore her vengeance. So she began her quest to find what the king valued most: his Black Diamond. What people didn't know was that the Black Diamond wasn't what they looked for. Everybody watched the tournament, distracted, when the worst happened. Zena attacked with her power. Everyone that was there became spellbound. Taking the moment, she entered the castle, casting a spell on anyone she found on her way. Some, it looked like, were thrown into a magic mirror, and if we take too long to save them, they will be stuck in there for the rest of their lives. Zena looked all over for the Black Diamond but never found anything."

"And do you know where it is?" Cristina asked.

"But of course I know!"

They heard a noise coming from the door. It was Zena, who heard everything the woman had confessed. She got closer.

"So you do know where it is!" screamed Zena.

"It was with me all this time," she answered.

"How did you get it?"

"You did many bad things and destroyed many things for something you didn't even know. You prevented a lot of people from following their lives."

"What do I care about this?" said Zena. "I'm not here to hear one of your sermons."

"I raised you. You should have listened to my advice."

"If you don't give me the Black Diamond, you'll be locked in here for the rest of your lives. You'll never see daylight again."

"Your powers are ending," said the woman. "You should have listened to me and not been so ambitious. You'll end up really bad."

"Your threat doesn't scare me. Now tell me where it is! I need to find it!" screamed Zena.

"You can look as much as you want. If you find it, it'll be yours."

They searched all over the room but without success. It was like looking for a needle in the haystack.

"You are making fun of me!" complained Zena.

Suddenly, they saw something shining and ran to it. Zena got closer and attacked Cristina, thinking she had the diamond. Abel got in the middle of fight, holding Zena by the arms. She yelled, calling for her dragon, and it came furiously and made Abel release her arm. At this moment, she struck him and left him lying on the ground.

"Give me this!" screamed Zena.

"Never!"

Abel stood up a little dizzy and got behind Zena. The two of them started to fight.

"Let's see if you can beat me, unless you decide to accept that invitation of mine. Do you remember it?" said Zena.

"Never! I'd prefer that you throw me into the mirror with the others!"

Zena felt even more humiliated. The prince's contempt was her worst defeat. But she insisted, "We'll have the world in our hands! Everything will be dominated by us. Everybody will bow down before us."

"I don't want any of this! I want the people's freedom!"

"Never!" Zena shouted angrily.

The dragon beside Cristina began to get furious and to breathe out fire. The woman, watching the scene, realized that the time had come for them to know the truth and yelled, "Black Diamond!"

And in front of Abel, a beautiful velvet-like black horse appeared. Abel mounted it and started to fight with the dragon again. Cristina watched the scene without knowing what to do. At that moment, she remembered the spear that Lady Lobélia had given her. The prince continued his fight with the dragon, but it looked like it was invincible. Cristina took the spear and threw it in the dragon's direction, nailing it in its heart.

The dragon let out a scream and started to disappear, fading in the air. At the same moment, Zena screamed, terrified, and instantly disappeared through the window.

In the last few minutes left to save the royal family, they ran, holding their hands, to be in front of the mirror. In that moment, the spell cast on the castle was undone. The people under the spell returned to what they were before. Some even considered the situation amusing.

"You were looking good as a broom," said the countess.

"You were funny as a chair," replied the other woman.

Laughter of happiness spread throughout the castle.

"You did it!" said the woman with a beautiful tiara on her head. And she touched and hugged the prince.

"Mother, I thought we couldn't do it!"

"It was hard to live cramped in that mirror," said the queen, smiling.

The king also appeared, thanking his son.

"Did you find my Black Diamond? No one has hurt him, right?"

A woman with a long-suffering face got to smile after some time.

"I took care of it all this time for you, sir."

"As always. You were loyal to me."

The king thanked her, promising to compensate her. Cristina felt happy with that scene. It seemed like a fairy tale where everything ended well. Suddenly, she saw a gray-haired man and a woman getting close.

"Mother! Father! Where were you?"

"On business," her father replied as he blinked at the woman next to him and continued. "You surprised me with your bravery and courage!"

"How do you know that, Dad?"

"We cheered for you all this time!"

"I found my biggest treasure now," she said, hugging them both and smiling happily.

"You are a great daughter!"

Later on, in the castle, everybody celebrated with a delicious dinner and with the sound of the choir composed by men and women dressed in black and white. Abel and Cristina talked on the castle's balcony.

They looked at the sky, and it seemed that someone was telling them, "There will always be a Zena to dominate the world and sacrifice its people. Many will believe their promises and will even carry her on their arms!"

Printed in the United States
By Bookmasters